So Happy!

By
KEVIN HENKES

Pictures by
ANITA LOBEL

Greenwillow Books
An Imprint of HarperCollinsPublishers

So Happy!
Text copyright © 2005 by Kevin Henkes
Illustrations copyright © 2005 by Anita Lobel
All rights reserved. Manufactured in China by
South China Printing Company Ltd.
www.harperchildrens.com

Watercolor paints and white gouache were
used to prepare the full-color art.
The text type is 20-point Barcelona Book.

Library of Congress Cataloging-in-Publication Data

Henkes, Kevin.
So happy! / by Kevin Henkes ; pictures by Anita
Lobel.
  p. cm.
"Greenwillow Books."
Summary: Brief text and illustrations tell the
story of a boy, a rabbit, and a seed.
ISBN 0-06-056483-0 (trade).
ISBN 0-06-056484-9 (lib. bdg).
(1. Seeds—Fiction. 2. Flowers—Fiction. 3. Rabbits—
Fiction.) I. Lobel, Anita, ill. II. Title.
PZ7.H389So 2005 (E)—dc22 2003056827

First Edition 10 9 8 7 6 5 4 3 2 1

 Greenwillow Books

For Anita—K. H.

For Kevin—A. L.

Someone had planted a magic seed.
The sun shone down,
but there was no rain,
so the seed didn't grow.

There was a little rabbit
who went out to explore.
He crossed the creek where it was
narrow as a ribbon.

He wandered

and wandered

until he didn't know where he was.

There was a little boy
who wanted something to do
but could think of nothing,
so he did just that.

The seed was thirsty.

The rabbit was lost.

The boy was bored.   Then . . .

The rain came.

The creek got bigger.

The seed started growing.

The boy got excited.

The rabbit was wet and scared.

The rain stopped.

The creek was wide as a door.

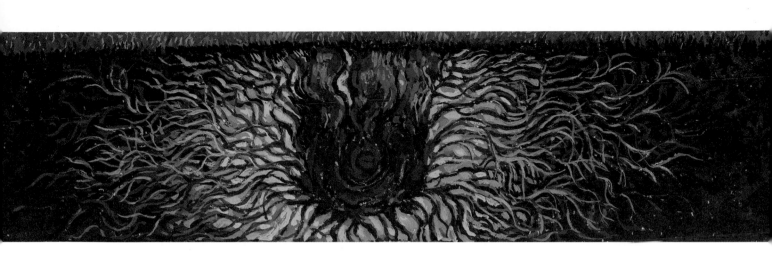

The seed was still growing.

The boy had an idea.

The rabbit couldn't get back across the creek.

The clouds broke up.

The creek sparkled and shone.

The seed poked through the ground.

The boy gathered sticks.
The rabbit raced about,
missing his mother.

The sky filled with birds.

The creek ran like a faucet.

The seed grew leaves and a bud.

The boy started to build.

The rabbit was too surprised to move.

A rainbow appeared.

The creek bubbled and hummed.

The seed was a flower.

The boy finished his bridge.

The rabbit crossed the creek.

The flower was ready.

The rabbit was home.

The boy was hungry.

Now the flower is gone.

The rabbit is asleep.

And the boy has a present for his mother.

So happy!